# Great-Grandmother's Treasure

by **Ruth Hickcox** ◆ pictures by **David Soman**

**Dial Books for Young Readers**  New York

For the babies of our babies:
Drew, Kristin, Adam, Jocelyn, Stephen, Holly, and Caleb—R.H.

For Dimitri, my beautiful new nephew—D.S.

Published by Dial Books for Young Readers
A member of Penguin Putnam Inc.
375 Hudson Street
New York, New York 10014

Library of Congress Cataloging in Publication Data
Hickcox, Ruth.
Great-Grandmother's treasure/by Ruth Hickcox; pictures by David Soman.
p. cm.
Summary: Great-Grandmother puts all the treasures of her life
into her apron and takes them with her when she dies.
ISBN 0-8037-1513-7.—ISBN 0-8037-1514-5 (lib. bdg.)
[1. Great-grandmothers—Fiction.] I. Soman, David, ill. II. Title.
PZ7.H525Gr 1998 [E]—DC20 93-42242 CIP AC

The art for this book was prepared using watercolors and pastels.

When Great-Grandmother was born, a bluebird sang.
Her mother and father held her close, and the bluebird sang of beginnings
and light.

Great-Grandmother was brand-new. She had nothing to remember,
and nothing to forget. Even her mother's smile was new, and the touch of
her blanket.

When Great-Grandmother was six, she found a rabbit in her father's rosebush. It looked frightened and hurt.

"Don't be afraid," Great-Grandmother whispered. "Look . . . I am little too." She gathered up the rabbit as gently as she could, and carried it into the house. "I will call you 'Sweet Rosebud,' and love you forever."

That night Sweet Rosebud slept in a pink, flowered hatbox. Great-Grandmother's father had lined it with grass. "Sure as God's in his heaven!" he said with surprise. "You are quite the doctor for six years old. Your rabbit is already eating its bed."

That was nothing. By morning the hatbox was a pile of pink paper. Some of the dollhouse steps were gone, and Sweet Rosebud was chewing a hole in the rug.

"That does it!" said Great-Grandmother's father. "Today we buy this rabbit a cage."

Now, Great-Grandmother loved Sweet Rosebud. She did not love cages. Cages were for locking tight, and keeping the wild things caught.

Once more Great-Grandmother gathered up her rabbit. This time it struggled hard to be free. "Don't be in such a hurry," she said through her tears. "Can't you see I want to love you just a little while more?"

When they reached the front lawn, Great-Grandmother gave Sweet Rosebud one last hug. Then the rabbit was gone.

When Great-Grandmother turned ten, her mother sat her down on the sofa. "It's high time you learned how to sew," she said. "And I think you should start with an apron."

It did not go well. Something kept bunching the stitches. The same thing kept knotting the thread.

"I'd rather be dancing!" Great-Grandmother complained. "Or running through butterfly fields." Then one day a needle fell into the oatmeal.

"That does it!" said Great-Grandmother's father.

It certainly did. There was no more talk about sewing.

When Great-Grandmother grew up, she fell in love with a soldier. The war was over, but not for him. It had been a bad war, as all wars are, and thoughts of the fighting were still in his head.

Great-Grandmother helped to change all that. She chased away the bad thoughts with laughter and singing and peanut butter cookies. They were married in the spring.

"Sure as God's in his heaven," Great-Grandmother then announced, "it's high time I made that apron."

It did not go well. But it went better than before, and this time Great-Grandmother put on pockets. A lot of them.

"Isn't it beautiful?" she said. "I can't believe I made it!"

Great-Grandfather thought it looked a little raggedy, but of course he did not say so.

"Someday," she said, "those pockets will be full. I'm going to fill them all with special treasure." Then she folded the apron carefully, and hid it away in a drawer.

On a quiet night, while a late winter snow was falling, their first baby was born. Great-Grandmother and Great-Grandfather held him close, and a new bird sang of beginnings and light.

After their fourth son was born, Great-Grandmother decided to put away her dollhouse. She learned how to play baseball instead. She also bought a book of very scary ghost stories. What she did with them was the talk of every child in town.

When Great-Grandmother told a ghost story, everything real came to a stop. Then slowly, like fog drifting in from the fields, the unreal began.

Windows shifted.  Doors slumped.  Shadows slipped right off the walls and out of the corners.

Great-Grandmother's ghosts were a miserable bunch.  That is what made them fun.  They moaned, and groaned, and made foolish faces.  One even turned inside out.  The worst ghost of all had a little trouble steering. He carried his head in a bag.  *That* was scary.  But Great-Grandmother always knew just when to stop.  "THE END!" she would say.  "The unreal is done."  And out came the peanut butter cookies.

All this time the apron lay folded in a
drawer.  The children found it one day when
they were playing.

"Mother!" they exclaimed.  "Where did
you get this apron?"

"It looks a little raggedy," said the
youngest.

Great-Grandmother smiled a mysterious
smile.  "I made it," she said, "and I'm going
to fill the pockets. Someday they'll all be full
of special treasure."  She folded the apron
carefully again, and placed it back in the
drawer.

Something awful happened when the four boys grew up. There was another war. This time Great-Grandfather was too old to fight. The sons became the soldiers. And this time the bad thoughts would not go away. Great-Grandmother had them too. She knew as she watched her boys leave home that she could not keep them safe.

And so she did what she always did when she could not help. She found a place where she could. Believe it or not, it was a place filled with cages. The cages were filled with dogs.

Great-Grandmother called them her "forgotten ones." They had nobody to love them, and no place to stay. The dogcatcher locked them up. "Don't you worry," she told them. "I will find you a home. I will dance when you are gone, because you will be free. And I will tie a pink balloon to your empty cage."

Great-Grandmother found a home for every single dog. She danced, and tied a pink balloon to each empty cage. Then she went looking for more new homes, because new forgotten ones kept arriving. She was very, very busy.

The war ended on a summery day when no one was expecting it. The grass smelled green again. The sky sounded blue. Great-Grandfather set off a fifty-firecracker explosion when the four boys came home.

The family began to grow like a tree in the garden. Great-Grandmother's babies had babies of their own. As with a tree, the branches kept spreading. There were grandbabies everywhere. Some of them were girls!

Great-Grandmother dusted off her dollhouse. Then she invited her oldest granddaughter to come to tea.

"Oh, Grandmother!" said the little girl. "What a beautiful dollhouse! But where are the steps? Some of them are gone."

"A friend of mine ate them," Great-Grandmother explained. Then she curled up with her grandchild in the big wing-chair, and they talked about Sweet Rosebud and the cage.

Every spring, after the first hard rain, Great-Grandmother gave a celebration. Only the grandchildren were invited, and Great-Grandfather of course.

"Oh, how I love the spring!" she would tell them. "Your grandfather and I were married in the spring. The puddles are at their very best, and the sun feels warm and new." Then they went celebrating.

What a mess! They celebrated every puddle in the neighborhood.

Water and mud flew all over the place, and the sun felt wonderfully
new. Nobody cared about soggy sneakers. No one worried about clean.
This was a party for splashes and messes. They kept on going until the
soup was done.

Great-Grandmother called it Mud Puddle Soup. It was really choco-
late pudding.

Those smart grandchildren knew all about the apron. They also knew something else: There was nothing in the pockets, not even a handkerchief.

"Grandmother!" they said. "Where is all your treasure? You must have a *mountain* of it by now."

Great-Grandmother smiled her mysterious smile. "I have treasure," she said, "but you cannot see it." Then she laughed so hard, she almost split her stockings. She would not tell them why.

Great-Grandmother became a great-grandmother when the babies of her babies began to have babies. Sure as God's in his heaven, she thought to herself, isn't this a hoot! Here I am, looking older than Philadelphia, but inside I am still exactly me. She did not think about it for very long, because there was too much to do. She still had homes to find for her dogs, and cookies to bake for the children.

Then slowly, like fog drifting in from the fields, the miseries began.

They were very real. Her ears stopped working, and she could not hear. Her teeth stopped working, and she could not chew. Her knees stopped working, and she could not dance. This was the hardest misery of all.

But my lap still works, she thought to herself. And my arms can hug. I am still a great-grandmother where it really counts.

Great-Grandfather died, during the winter snows. Great-Grandmother tied her last balloon to the arm of his empty chair. And when Great-Grandfather left, a piece of her went with him. It was the piece that loved the spring.

Nobody talked about the apron anymore.

In fact, everyone had forgotten all about it. The treasure had never been found.

For the first time since anyone could remember, Great-Grandmother had nothing to do. She had gone from hurry to stop. Day after day, week after week, she sat in the old wing-chair. The family was concerned.

They needn't have worried. Great-Grandmother was sitting at a picnic. It was a picnic in her mind. She had spread her memories all around her, like a feast on a red-checked cloth. She was tasting them, one by one.

Sometimes she was a little girl again, running through butterfly fields. Sometimes she was rocking one of her babies.

And sometimes, sometimes Great-Grandfather came by. He would take her hand and they would go walking together, back through the early spring.

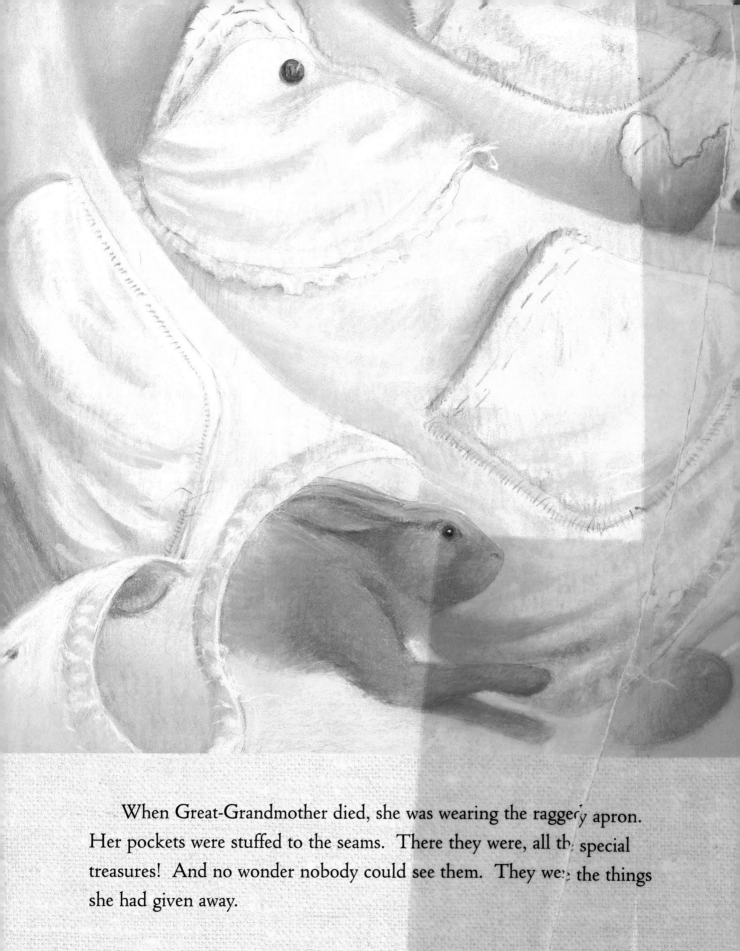

When Great-Grandmother died, she was wearing the raggety apron. Her pockets were stuffed to the seams. There they were, all the special treasures! And no wonder nobody could see them. They were the things she had given away.

There were smiles of course, and peanut butter cookies, ghost stories and Mud Puddle Soup, dollhouse families, books, baseball games in summer, empty cages, and pink balloons. In the very smallest pocket was the earliest gift of all: the hug for a rabbit going free.

When Great-Grandmother died, her bluebird sang.  Slowly she began
to dance, while the bluebird sang of beginnings and light.
Just as sure as God is in his heaven, she is dancing still.